ARROYO

Lisa Gonzales

Introduced by Helena María Viramontes

© 2004 by Lisa Gonzales

Introduction © 2004 by Helena María Viramontes
Cover art © 2004 by Puni Kukahiko

Printed in the United States of America
First Edition

All rights reserved

Book design by Kathleen Culla and Charles Valle

Logo design by Susan Jones
Web design by Cheryl Kelly

ISBN: 0-9710465-5-7

Momotombo Press
Francisco Aragón, Editor
María Meléndez, Associate Editor
Richard Yañez, Associate Editor
Cristina Gutierrez, Editorial Assistant
www.momotombopress.com
editor@momotombopress.com

Momotombo Press, newly housed at the Institute for Latino Studies at the University of Notre Dame, strives to promote emerging voices in Latino Literature in the chapbook format—specifically, those writers who have yet to publish a full-length collection of their work. For more information, visit our website at www.momotombopress.com
or contact Francisco Aragón at: faragon@nd.edu   Or write:

Francisco Aragón
Institute for Latino Studies
230 McKenna Hall
University of Notre Dame
Notre Dame, IN 46556

Contents

Editor's Note   5

Introduction   6

I

Arroyo   10

The Hawaiian Band   19

II

Love in the Blood   24

Acknowledgements   31

Author profile   32

Editor's Note

Chatting over lunch, talk turns to identity politics vis-à-vis the Chicano Chapbook Series. Richard Yañez and I are co-editing an anthology based on it. We agree that Gary Soto, by publishing Jim Sagel, seemed to be suggesting that being of Mexican descent was not a strict requirement for inclusion. Our pending anthology is "based" on the Series because we want to remedy the dearth of women who benefited from Soto's vision: we intend to publish a number of emerging Latina writers whose work we admire, but who did not have a chapbook published. Then Lisa Gonzales, also at the table, says, "Would someone like *me* fit in?..."

We learn that Gonzales grew up in Fairfield, California; that Catholicism was a pillar in her home; that she was the youngest of six siblings; that she was certain of one thing: she wasn't white. We learn that listening to her mother's stories formed an indelible part of her childhood; stories that included migration…but not migration from, for example, Michoacán to Bakersfield—but rather: migration from Portugal to Hawaii, from the Philippines to Hawaii. And we learn that with these stories shimmering inside her, Lisa Gonzales' desire to write was stirred by reading *The House on Mango Street,* and *Drown*.

When I began to read her work in 2002 I was immediately taken by its lyricism—the work's appeal to the senses, its attention to nuance of gesture when shaping characters. Until then, I had only enjoyed what she had read aloud at readings at UC Davis. It was a delight, therefore, to experience how moved I was by her art—on the page.

When our book based on the Chicano Chapbook Series fell through, Gonzales became, in my mind, a Momotombo author. And yet I know some will perhaps question her presence here. To them I say: I opt for a spirit of inclusion. Her voice very much speaks to my sensibility as a Latino, adding to that strand of our literature that brings to life our family histories, with all their joys…and all their sadness. Momotombo Press, whose mission is to promote emerging Latino/a writers, is proud to mark its new home by publishing Lisa Gonzales.

Francisco Aragón
Institute for Latino Studies
University of Notre Dame

Introduction

by Helena María Viramontes

I do not know much about the writer Lisa Gonzales. A resume only summarizes accomplishments in a hollow sense, never giving us the gut and gristle of a person. All I have to behold, to admire, to feel astonished by, is her collection of three stories titled *Arroyo*. In the title story, Teresa, the narrator is a very young girl who lives in a neighborhood in Hawaii where people speak Portuguese, though she is considered a haole because of her anglo father. "Your father is not a bad man" the narrator's mother tells her after her father kills the neighbor boy by running him over. The father's disdain for this community, as well as for the blood that pulses in his own daughter, is something that she feels but hasn't the language to describe. In fact, in this beautifully lyrical story, the unspoken is louder than words— the muted characters in this particular situation can't find the words to describe tragedy and Gonzales' style becomes as powerful as any Mary Robison or Raymond Carver story.

In "The Hawaiian Band" the narrator lives near Teresa and her family, but this time the narrator is a tough minded fourteen year old, made tough by her impoverished circumstances and her family life. The "Hawaiian Band" contains irony—whenever the children get beaten by uncles or aunts, they put the radio on real loud to drown out the childrens' cries. In a twist of sisterhood, the narrator and her younger sister, Ruby (who also appears in "Arroyo," suggesting that Gonzales is working on interconnected stories) takes command of their situation by literally fighting back. There is no sentimentality or false epiphanies. Just a simple recognition of love between the sisters which acts as a physical shield against the harshness of their reality. Again the first person singular gives us a sense of otherworldliness, intriguing, heartbreaking but ultimately hopeful.

Finally, we have a tour de force story, reminiscent of early Alice Walker. In "Love in the Blood" Gonzales' narrator is an older woman having seen hardships which would break most of us in two. Yet, in her own words, almost as if the reader is listening to a testimonio, we hear her speak of her life as it revolves around her adopted son, a nephew, leading to a scene of complete and total sorrow. The nuanced language, the speaker's observations, her loving way with her nephew makes a reader's heart ache for some relief for this woman. And yet she is one that never feels sorry for herself. Indeed, she carries herself with a sense of dignity that is totally appropriate for a heart spun of gold. Simply a remarkable story.

There is nothing more exciting than discovering a rising light in American literature. No doubt, the work of Lisa Gonzales will shine bright. It already dazzles.

*to my first storyteller
whose memory reaches back generations
—toda a família atrás da casa.*

I

Arroyo

On the day my father killed the neighbor boy, my mother took me upstairs, undressed me, and put my clothes in a trash bag. I stood naked in the bathroom, arms at my side, and tried to settle my thoughts, flatten them out, make my mind as smooth as the white-tiled floor.

She turned on the water and helped me into the bathtub, holding my hand to keep me from a hard slip on porcelain. I slid my legs under the warm water. The coldness on the soles of my feet floated away and I bent forward, folding myself into the rising bath.

Quiet, quiet, quiet, I thought.

"Your father is not a bad man," my mother said while rubbing the bar of soap over a stiff bristle brush. She began to cry.

I stared at the water pounding down from the faucet and thought of my father in the back of the police car, driving away without ever looking back at us.

"Your father is not a bad man," she said, this time with more force, and continued to scrub me with hard strokes until my skin was pink. She dried me off with a thick towel and wrapped it around me twice. She powdered my body, put me in a fresh dress and braided my wet hair.

I followed her into the master bedroom and sat down on their bed, running my fingers along the nubly chenille bedspread. She changed out of her yellow dress ruined by a copper stain at the lap.

Walking out of our front yard, we made the sign of the cross for the soul of little Arthur Arroyo as we skirted the child-size blotch of blood. Around the edges, the sun was changing the stain from red to a dark dullness like air hardening lava.

My father drove right up on Arthur—the deaf boy's eyes shiny—and left the car's engine running like a heater that won't stop heating.

   We crossed Seventh Avenue to the old vovo's house. The chickens were making a racket in the backyard. Even though other houses kept fowl, my father only complained about hers.
   "They live like pigs," my father had said. Mrs. Cruze lived in a small house across the street from us with some of her children and grandchildren. The tone of his voice made me want to disagree even though I wasn't sure what he was talking about. Their yard was just as neat as anyone else's even with the chickens and all the old vovo's parties.
   "And those kids. Who knows who they belong to." He paused to bite the end off his cigar, his teeth sliding through the tobacco skin.
   "They're Marileide's—" said my mother.
   He puffed on the cigar until a gray haze settled above his head. "I mean the father," he said. Then another stream of smoke, the thick fumes spreading throughout the room.

The old vovo's eyes were brown but cloudy as if spider webs covered them, and her shaking hand bumped me as she reached for my shoulder. Her arms looked like dimpled loaves of dough tucked into the sleeves of her muumuu. I had never been so close to her.
   We walked into a big, shady room with an upright piano—someone played it nearly every night—and rooster figurines everywhere. Most were black, others blue or white, and each with a flared, red crest standing straight up on its head.
   I tried to move quietly quietly through the room, but I couldn't keep my sandals from crunching on the tatami mats.

   "What for to eat?" the old vovo asked. We sat down on a red sofa with cushions bumpy like the skin of unripe tamarinds.
   "Oh no. No thank you, Mrs. Cruze," my mother said.

"Of course you eat, Isabel. How some oranges, cookies, mangos?" My mother shook her head to each.

The old vovo began to speak in Portuguese. I hadn't heard these sounds since my avô died. My father didn't speak the language and didn't want me to either. I knew only a few words—pequeninha for little one, rabicho for pigtail, lesão for bruise.

My mother took my hand and patted it lightly. I didn't need to talk or even listen, just sit quietly. Their words sounded like small coughs.

She began to cry. I took my hand away from hers and picked up a small pillow. I traced the rooster's comb with the tip of my pointing finger. I tried to only think about the bird—the fringe of each feather, the sharp spikes of his claws—and not my mother's strange voice or Arthur on the curb outside my house or what my father would do when he found out my mother and I were in the Cruze house.

"You like my roosters, eh?"

I paused, my fingernail slicing through soft red thread, unsure if she was speaking English or if it was only my imagination.

"My roosters, do you like?" the old vovo asked again. I nodded.

"In Portugal, they lucky. This you know?" I shook my head.

"Now you know," she said and stretched her arm out in front of her. "See how lucky my house is?"

"You stay here until I come for you, Teresa," my mother said. I wanted to be home in my room. I thought about how I never broke my father's rules. She moved her hand along the side of my cool face. "You can play with Ruby and Madra."

Sometimes I watched the two girls from across the street. Mostly I watched Madra—playing jacks with Arthur, walking with her mother from the bus stop, singing and dancing on her porch like it was a stage.

"She fine, Isabel," the old vovo said. "We sit, we talk. You go now." My mother walked away from me and out the door, ladders of gray scuffs along the back of her round heels.

I stared down at the pillow, wondering what the old vovo could see of me—me on the couch right then or me other times watching her from my window. The torches that ringed her late-night parties made her yard look like the fire craters I learned about in school—how they would light up Diamond Head so that the kānaka canoeing in from the other islands could find their way.

She made some noises, a few groans and clicks of her tongue. I didn't look up.

My father said Arthur was deaf and dumb, but my mother said he wasn't dumb, just slow. He was the second oldest of seven kids. He lived down the street from me. He had a hard time playing fast games. He always wanted the ball no matter where he was in the game. He would sit on the curb in front of my house where my father would park. Arthur kept his hands along the side of his face, shading his eyes from the sun.

"Ruby!" she shouted. My head snapped back like when my father yanks on my braid. The old vovo smiled at me, her grin showing her red gums and deepening every wrinkle.

Ruby ran in from the backyard, slamming the screen door so hard that all the little statues seemed to shiver. She wore a faded blue dress pulling apart at the buttons along her belly. She trotted into the room and stopped short.

Arthur would sit on the curb outside my house. His voice made words seem round. "Hi Teresa," he said. He turned and gave me a small wave. I was still in my church clothes and patent leather shoes, walking stiffly on my porch so that my

13

heels made loud sharp clicks.

"What's the haole doing here?" Ruby asked, her hands on her straight hips.

"Hush it, menina," the old vovo said. "Little sister gonna stay awhile, so be nice. You two gonna go out and feed my galinhas."

I looked at each crease of the woman's face, and stopped on three hairs growing out of a small brown mole on her chin.

We walked along a narrow path lined by blooming hibiscus hedges, each blood-red flower spread wide open. The backyard was big with a chicken coop in the corner—a rickety shack with a rusty tin roof and gaps around the sides like missing teeth.

Chickens gathered at our feet as soon as we started tossing the feed onto the dirt. I tried to count them. The birds seemed faded and blurry compared to the statues in the old vovo's house.

I jumped and let out a yelp when one of the roosters pecked my foot.

"Don't stand in the middle of their food, stupid," Ruby said. "Haven't you ever fed chickens before?" I stepped out from their feed. They were so small, and I thought that maybe if my father got up close to these chickens he might not hate them so much. I reached into the bag and took out a handful.

"Where's your dad?" Ruby asked.

I made a bony-shouldered shrug and looked up at Ruby. Her cheeks and nose were always bright red from the sun. I thought of running back home to my mother where I could rest my hot face against the softness of her belly.

I didn't know what happened when the police took someone away, and there was no one for me to ask.

"Where's *your* dad?" I asked.

She looked at me and became still, her arm stretched in front of her. Chicken feed trickled out of the corner of her fist like water. When she moved again, it was to turn her body away from me. She flung her arm and scattered the feed far away from us. Over her shoulder I could see the flat crest of Diamond Head in the distance.

"My mom once met Shirley Temple," Ruby said, her chin pointing upward. "She stayed at the Royal Hawaiian and my mom said she was like a perfect little doll." Ruby put down the feed pail. She walked over to the grass and began to twirl, her dress billowing out around her legs. I did the same, twisting my feet around and stretching my arms out.

"My mom said she was just as sweet as in the movies," Ruby said in fits while becoming short of breath.

The twirling slowed until we fell back onto the ground, squawking chickens scattering around us. I closed my eyes, but I still felt the spinning, and from out of it I could see Arthur sitting on the curb in front of my house—the back of his neck sweating, the ends of his damp hair gathered into black spikes. I caught my breath and opened my eyes.

"What about Madra?" I said, rolling over onto my side toward Ruby, so close my breath was on her shoulder.

"She's in our room with the door closed," Ruby said. Madra liked to sing fast songs and walk with bottle caps stuck in the soles of her shoes.

Ruby sat up and ran her fingers along the lawn, cutting furrows into the ground. Then she brushed her hands together, dropping bits of feed and soil onto the front of her dress.

I lay back down and watched the clouds as they moved mauka from Waikiki and made the air feel thick and wet. I closed my eyes but I could still see them moving behind my eyelids and feel their water in my breath.

The smell of curry came from inside the house. The sun was going down and I hadn't eaten anything since breakfast. I walked to the screen door of the old vovo's kitchen. Ruby's mom, Marileide, was sitting at the table talking with the old vovo. I thought I'd ask her about Shirley Temple, but instead stayed quiet.

"That Hanson. What a crazy bugger," Marileide said. Her deep voice made each word sound like a rumble. "Isabel knew about him."

"Hush it now. The girl might hear," the old vovo said.

Once at the screen door of the Arroyos' house, I watched Mrs. Arroyo feed the three youngest children. She squatted on the family room floor with a bowl of poi, the children sitting in a half-circle around her. She dipped two fingers into the poi like a spoon, then flipped her fingers into their waiting mouths, one right after the other. I never went back.

"What an animal to do this thing," Marileide said, and I wanted then to run across the street into my own house and up the stairs to my bedroom, but the thought of seeing Arthur's dried blood made me shiver and kept me from leaving. Then all the times my father told me to never go over to the old vovo's house came to me, and I didn't know where I should be and thought that maybe I didn't belong anywhere.

"What would make a man do that?" Marileide said. I squeezed my hands into fists and waited. I tilted my head toward the screen door and held my breath so I wouldn't miss a word of the old vovo's answer.

"Who can know what a mind think?" the old vovo said. She leaned back in the chair and wiped at her eyes with a frayed dishtowel. "The boy still dead."

I let my breath out slowly and without sound, not to keep listening but just to stay quiet, to make that moment and everything in it still and calm like when I float on my back in the shallow water at Ala Moana, not moving and my arms outstretched, my ears just below the surface and filled with silence.

I looked up. I thought the kitchen would be empty, but the old vovo and Marileide were still there at the table and they were quiet, too.

"I'm going to go check on Madra, then I'll go down to the Arroyos," Marileide said. She got up and hugged the old vovo then kissed her on the top of her head. Marileide looked at me standing at the door, and I had no doubt that she could see what piece of my father lived in me.

I wanted to tell her that I didn't know what I enjoyed most when he would drive up to Arthur sitting in his parking space—seeing him honk at Arthur, his stomping back up to the house, or his face becoming redder and puffier like a raising welt—and that watching him made me feel a bigness grow like when I have a secret, not one that's been told to me but one that I've found out for myself.

"Why don't you come in and eat," Marileide said. She looked past me to Ruby lying on the lawn. Then she took a plate of food and walked out of the kitchen down the hallway, and I pictured her going into Madra's room, sitting next to her daughter and petting Madra's shiny, shiny brown hair.

I wasn't hungry, but the old vovo insisted that I have a little bit of sweet potato. Alone at the table, I heard Marileide leave for the Arroyos and their small white house with floors of gray stone.

17

After I ate the sweet potato, I went into the living room. The lamp didn't give off much light, but I could see a black rooster statue with blue and red feathers painted on its sides. I looked over my shoulder, then picked it up. The bird was made of wood and felt heavier than I thought it would be. I put it on the ledge of the picture window and tapped its beak against the pane.

Outside, the sun was down, and I could smell the light mist from the Palolo Valley carried out by the trades. I glanced up from the rooster and saw movement across the street. On her knees my mother was scrubbing the sidewalk in front of our house.

I stroked the crest of the rooster. Her back arched as she stretched forward and back, her arms moving back and forth. A stream of water ran away from her and down the sloping street. I felt something crack inside of me then—like how my eardrums pop when coming down off the Pali—and I began to cry.

I took another look around the room, grabbed the rooster and put it in my pocket. I walked to the door.

"Little sister."

The voice came from behind me. I turned around.

"My dad's not a bad man," I said, my hand squeezing the rooster through the thin fabric of my dress. Slowly the old vovo moved toward me and stretched her arm straight out in front of her body, her shaking palm turned upward. I looked into her webbed eyes.

I reached into my pocket to take out the statue, but instead she placed her hand on my shoulder. She pulled me in close and spoke to me so softly I couldn't tell in what language. I kept my hand in my pocket, my fingers moving over the rooster's warm red crest.

The Hawaiian Band

When I laugh about the Hawaiian Band with my sister, Ruby, we're not laughing about music, although there was plenty of music in our house, and not just from the radio because Ruby and I would sing in harmony. I played the piano—so did our Auntie Lally, her painted fingernails clicking the keys like chips of red bone—and we would sing nearly every night, or have big festas in the front yard where my old avó would play the mandolin so lightly that the music and the breeze seemed to be one, drifting over our bodies in the dark.
    No. We say the Hawaiian Band plays when someone turns the radio up to drown the hollers of a child getting lickings. The Band plays for us many times, like when we come home from the beach red and blistered, and we know we're not supposed to go by ourselves because they tell us the ocean is dangerous, that we might sink or step on a man-of-war. But how can we resist when the sun is warm and the smell of my old avó cooking bacalhau waters our eyes and brings every fly in the neighborhood to our screens. We just want to go, and we're kids, so we go.
    We stay at the beach all day. Don't even need bathing suits, just ourselves and some mock oranges or mangos we pinch from the verdura man, and then we're at the beach having good fun. No such thing as sunscreen in our time, just the sand, our skin, the sun, and the water blue and us red. When we go back home, we say, "No, we didn't go to the beach," while our wet clothes hang on the clothesline dripping salt water onto the gardenias. My avó doesn't know since she's blind and she's just happy we're home, but when Uncle John comes home he gives us lickings, then Auntie Lally and we get more lickings, and then Ma last, and I do feel bad because she's so tired from work.
    Auntie Lally's the worse of them all with her koa stick—termites can't eat koa, so you know the wood's hard—and she makes the stick special for us. She takes it to work and sands it

smooth, drills a hole in one end where she ties a strip of leather to hang on a nail by the back door. The stick is brown and dark, and Auntie Lally may be one big woman, but she's quick. We try to run by her when we come through the door, but she grabs her stick and we all get cracks, hard and sharp, on the backs of our heads. And I laugh now when I think of Lally, fast and fat, or how we're so dumb we don't even think to go through the front door.

We all hear the Hawaiian Band play, but I get the most lickings when I bring home ukus from Amy Arroyo's house. There's Ma picking out the nits from my head, running her fingernails along each strand of my brown hair while I sit on the floor between her swollen feet. She crouches over me after she's crouched over beds and bathtubs all day at work, and with each uku she picks, I get a hard croque on my head. I holler with each knock of her knuckle, and when she's done I wash my sheets with lye so strong the soap burns my cuticles like heated glass. I say, "No, I won't go to Amy's anymore," but she's my best friend, so how can I resist? Then it starts all over and the Hawaiian Band plays while I get good lickings, and I have to laugh now that I know what it's like to have kids with no sense.

So when we girls get older, Ma tells the uncles no more Hawaiian Band because by now they're drinking more and the whiskey either makes them sing or makes them mean. Ma stands her ground with her brothers the best she can, but she works most nights, and the uncles get sick of the kids in the house. So one day—I'm fourteen—I come home late from playing volleyball. Uncle and his friends are still trying to dig a basement under the house—that basement never does get finished because the shoveling stops when the whiskey arrives—and Uncle's drunk and mad at me when I walk through the door because I wasn't home to do the dishes.

Uncle grumbles something at me—he's always grumbling—and I walk on by him because my hands hurt from spiking the volleyball, and I don't want to do the dishes anyway. So I go into my bedroom and lie on my bed when I hear the smooth sound of the Harry Owens Orchestra begin to rise from the radio in the living room. Ruby's on her bed and I'm on mine, lying on my stomach with my back to the door. We look at each other without speaking the way sisters do when they're waiting together for what's coming next.

Uncle John appears in the doorway and says, "Who's going to do those dishes?"

"You do them," I say, and I can't believe those words came out, that my words sneak around on me just like I do on my uncle. Ruby's just as surprised, and she puts her hand over her mouth to cover her smile.

The orchestra plays "Sweet Leilani"—*Sweet Leilani/ Heavenly flower/ I dream of paradise for two*—and I hear Uncle John whip off his belt, that dark leather belt so thin it snaps when he uses it like the strap is made just for giving us dirty beatings.

I lie still on my bed, thinking that Ma laid down the law so he won't give me any more lickings, when I hear the high-pitched hum of the strap through the air, then the snap of the belt on my back, and it might as well have been a knife for the sharp cut of pain the belt slices on my skin. I scream, my voice higher than the whip of his strap and the rush of the woodwinds, and I don't even stop as Ruby jumps off her bed and pushes Uncle John into the wall and hollers, "Crack him, Madra!"

I get up quick from my bed. I look into Uncle's brown eyes that look at me and see nothing, and a feeling begins to burn inside me. The heat in my back grows, flows through my body until my skin is red and I feel filled with it. My tears dry and I see Uncle so clearly like my whole body has eyes. I make a fist and punch him in the side of his face.

Uncle John stumbles to the floor in stages, each part of his body making its own low thump, and I think now that he falls more from the whiskey than my fist. Uncle's bleeding on the tatami mats and hollering at everyone, but all I hear is the radio—the steel guitar, the clear soprano voice.

Soon the whole família is at the doorway looking in at the three of us, all of them quiet except for my old avó's clicking, her tongue tapping out the drift of her thoughts. Ruby and I grab each other's arms and stand over Uncle, but we don't look down at him. We just look at each other, standing in our room with our arms locked together, blinking like our eyes are new.

II

Love in the Blood

This house, it mine. Papa come to O'ahu in 1882, take a boat from Lisbon and they at sea for two months. He a teacher in Portugal, but when he get here, he work three years in the cane to pay his passage. He say the workers all live in little shacks. Nothing but one room with straw mats on the floor to sleep. The men just work and drink, and Papa say they harsh, more like dogs than men. Once he paid off, he work for a year, then send for my mama. Five more years and he buy this land, build this house.

I the only one left now, so this house mine. I seven when mama pass on while she birthing Anthony. Me and little sister stay in our room, pull the white sheet over our heads, try to only think about the smell of gardenias in the bedsheets, but still we hear mama's screams. She call out to the Virgin. Scream Hail Marys like she think the Virgin deaf. Then the house quiet for a long time. Make me think like when I go out back to the corn patch. Lay myself down between the stalks so still, no moving except for the cornsilk in the wind. Maybe I hear flies or a cricket, but mostly just quiet.

The midwife open the door. She call me out, need my help. We just girls, so we scared. Little sister grab my arm and say, "Don't leave me alone." I don't want to go, don't want to leave Rosalie. I pull the sheet back over my head, but the midwife say I gotta go, so I do.

"Where Papa?" I say.

"He at work," she say.

"Where Mama?"

The midwife stay silent, just take my hand and walk me to Mama's room. The sun slant through the window, make the room so gold and hot. The first time I see little brother, he in the egg basket on the floor. He all wrapped in a blanket and he cry real loud.

"Where Mama?" I ask. I don't see nothing but a covered lump on the bed, and I think the lump too small to be Mama.

The midwife tell me, "Take brother out. He need to be fed."

I take him to the kitchen, make him a thin gruel of corn flour and goat milk. I feed him and think I never see Mama again. But that night she come to me. Not her whole self, just her voice. I in bed when I hear her so close to my face like she my pillow. Real soft, she whisper, "You the mama now."

That all she say. I want more words. I want to know why she leave and what I do now. Maybe I want to hear the song she sing in Portuguese when she take an egg from a hen. She gone though, and there no more songs.

Everything I say the truth. I an old woman and got no need to lie. Mama come to me that night. Maybe she visit all the family 'cause they know I the new mama. At first, the aunties come give help, then no one but me.

I never think my hands so quick and strong, but I take care of all. I wash little sister's hair. I clean and cook. Scrub the clothes with lye until my knuckles raw. Even name little brother. I think a week too long without a name, so I say "Anthony" and then he have a name.

A house need a little boy. Thirty years after Anthony I got another boy. Born to little sister, but still he mine.

And that boy, he move slow. I always saying "Daniel, move faster" or "Do this now." He slow, but he good. He listen to his auntie. I say, "Milk them goats," and he do. He take his own comb and use it on their stiff hair when he think I don't see.

Daniel love them dirty animals. He got a bantam rooster that come when he whistle, that fly onto the ground from the breadfruit tree and follow him like a dog. That boy, he name the bantam Spike. I laugh hard the first time I hear that.

When my man—he dead now—see the rooster's trick, he want the cock for himself. We together for twenty years and he think I gonna let him take the boy's rooster to the cockfight, bring it back to the boy all cut and bloody. I keep my man from the bird, tell him plain the bantam belong to the boy. He try to scare me, take his fist and pound the table, but I got no fear of him. I lift my iron skillet over my head and slam it on that fist. He holler from pain, maybe surprise, too. But he got another hand, and his punch knock me back to the wall, then I fall on the floor. I spit out blood and a yellow tooth, hold it up for my man to see. He shut up about the rooster.

I know Daniel before he even born. Rosalie's belly big. She carry low and forward. I put my hands on her belly and I see his black hair, the shape of his fist. I tell little sister, "You got a boy." I know this not what she want to hear, but it what I see.

She say, "No, I already got four. Now I need a girl around the house."

I got none of each, so I say, "Give him hanai to me if he a boy," and she do. Her husband, Santiago, not happy at all. He want the boy in his house. He say that a son's a son, but Rosalie got a beauty way and he know he lucky with her. Santiago a man in love and that enough to give up his flesh and blood.

I stay with Rosalie for the birthing, put black rosary beads around her neck and squeeze her hand. When it time, the boy come bloody and fierce, split through his mama's legs like an ax on heartwood. When I hear him the first time, his voice not a whimper, but a howl. His open mouth shiver, and I see one white tooth stick out his bottom gum.

We all in shock to see his tooth. The midwife make the sign of the cross, think that tooth mean he got the wild boar spirit. She try to put the evil eye on the boy, so I smack her hard across the face. The midwife run out and leave me and Rosalie with the baby.

"What his name?" Rosalie ask me.

"Daniel," I say.

So I got myself a boy, but Rosalie don't make it easy. She keep the boy from me for six months. I go see him every week. I say, "I ready for him." I hold Daniel, cradle him in my lap and know he mine. In my arms, he fit me just right. I look down at him and think, "He a marvel." The want I have for him grow in me so big until my breath come short. It time for the boy to come home to me. No reason for Rosalie to keep him when he don't take the breast. His tooth cut her nipple from the start, then her milk all dry up.

I know it a harsh thing for a mama to give up her boy. I see the way she look at him. But I got a look, too. She know this. She saw my look when Anthony leave me, go to fight the first war and never come back. She know my loss. She got five boys. I got none. She know what fair.

"He come visit us," she say. "I want him to know his brothers."

"That fair," I say.

She wrap him in a sheet and put him in a basket. I start the walk home. When I down the road, she holler out to me.

"Remember," she shout, "you only his auntie."

That boy, he in my house. I never know how a babe get so dirty, and I wash him every night in a small tin basin, heat the water on the stove, make sure it just right. I clean red dirt from his little gold body. After he can walk, I teach him to feed the chickens. He low to the ground and it just come natural. Then he learn to tend the goats. That boy, he suck milk from their teats if I let him. Soon, he picking mangos and dates and corn. But nothing like he with the animals. He talk to them, give them all names, and I see he know his own way of doing things. He slow, but he work.

We mostly happy. I don't count on his Filipino blood though. Daniel got a temper quick as the rains. Like when one of them goats don't mind, the boy turn red as new blood and give the goat a push. At first my man think Daniel's temper cute, but then he use the belt. He whip the boy fierce when they fight over the breadfruit tree. He want to chop it down, say we need the wood, but the boy don't want to lose the tree.

27

"That tree mine," Daniel say, his voice so big.

"Nothing here yours," my man say so easy like he cutting into a peach.

I see what coming next, but I stay silent, think Daniel need to learn to fight more than his goats. The boy start running, charge his uncle when he see the ax. My man land hard on the red earth so he almost fall on the blade. He scared to see the ax so close, and he let the breadfruit tree stand, but my man still give Daniel a dirty beating.

I know my man not happy about the boy, that when he look at the boy, he only see my dead womb flat and gray like ash. But that boy mine and I say, "No more whipping." My man stop, but every now and then, when the boy show his temper, he say under his breath, "Filipino stick knife." Like I never hear this saying before. I tell little sister the same when I first see Santiago. But love, it don't know blood.

That boy, he ten when his mama die. She not sick, and we never know what happen. Just one day little sister don't wake up, and then she gone. Daniel look up at me with his eyes black as a crow's wing and ask, "Auntie, why my mama die?" I got no words to tell a boy about death and all that means.

"My mama die when I little, too," I say, but that no comfort and he don't ask any more questions.

I dress him in a white shirt and black short-pants for the funeral Mass. We go to Rosalie's grave at the foot of Diamond Head, stand next to her koa casket. The wind blow hard that day, and I think about us two sisters under a white sheet forty years ago. How our mama plant gardenias under the clothesline where our linen hang dry and we fall asleep in their sweetness.

Now I got Rosalie's boy at my side. I squeeze his little hand, feel the soft blisters on his palm. His papa and brothers on the other side of his mama's box, they stare at me and the boy. I want to push him behind me, but suddenly he hard and

heavy.
   The boy look just like a little man, try to keep the tears back. He don't know a boy need to cry at his mama's grave, and he seem shy when the tears come. He bend his head into the crook of his arm, and his whole body start to roll like the tide.
   That night Daniel's papa come to my house. Santiago a big man with a chest like a whiskey barrel, and I see why my sister have so many children.
   "Papa," Daniel say and run out to us from his room. Santiago pick up the boy easy, make me think how long it been since I do that now he so big. I stand and watch the two of them and feel like I looking into a house through a window.
   "Go play with your rooster," the boy's papa say. "I gonna talk to your auntie."
   When the boy leave, it just me and Santiago and my man around the kitchen table. I see that maybe Santiago come to say something I don't want to hear.
   I look down and see he walk red mud all over my floor. I tell him, "I always cleaning up your mess."
   He say, "I want my boy." Just like that. Like ten years nothing but a wind. My man leave the room, leave me alone like he always do.
   "But that boy, he mine," I say. I scared now. My belly start to twist and feel like it full of snakes. "I raise him, I learn him, I take care of him."
   The boy's papa move forward until his face so close, his breath burn my eyes. He say slow, "I'm taking my boy," and I see where the boy got his temper. My face feel so hot like I at the stove.
   I swallow hard and say, "But we got a deal."
   He say, "Your deal buried at Diamond Head," and I know I got no chance with him. The boy out in my yard playing with the bantam, but he already gone.
   I go to Daniel's room. Pack his things in a denim duffel

bag. I think there ought to be more after ten years, but the clothes as small as the boy and don't take up much space. I know Santiago will throw out the clothes. He want to start over, get the boy new things, but still I pack. I got no use for little boy clothes.

The boy tell me goodbye, put his brown arms around my neck. But he don't squeeze, just let them lay there. Then he gone, and I think about little sister, how she want me to know that I the boy's auntie. How once she scared to be alone, and how I leave while she hide under the bedsheets. I think these things all at the same time, like when a hard wind blow down a mountain crater and spin around so you don't know which way the wind come.

After Daniel leave, I keep the bantam for awhile. Then one day I catch the bird. It not easy when the rooster so quick. Grab it by the throat and hold it down on a stump. The bantam fight me like it know what gonna come next, flap its wings, even get a piece of my skin. In my arm it catch me good, take a chunk of flesh that it spit out on the ground.

My blood drip down on the stump. The bantam's crow turn into a scream, but it don't give in, even keep fighting after the ax come down on its neck. I take its bloody head from the stump while its body run around the yard, then bury the head under the breadfruit tree.

When the body of the bantam lose its fight, I clean the bird. Hard to pluck its feathers when it so old. I throw its guts to the goats and save its feet to make my soup thick. Not much meat on the bone, so I don't eat any, just feed it to my man. The flesh, it tough and stringy, but he don't care. He eat the carcass clean, even suck on the dry bones. I don't tell him he eating the bantam.

Acknowledgements

"The Hawaiian Band" first appeared in *in*tense* and "Love in the Blood" first appeared in *The Chattahoochee Review*

*

For support of this project, I wish to thank the Jacob K. Javits Foundation of the U.S. Department of Education, the East-West Center at the University of Hawaii at Manoa, the Institute for Latino Studies at the University of Notre Dame, and Francisco Aragón.

For their help in shaping these three stories, obrigado to my teachers—Katherine Vaz, James Houston, Jack Hicks, Clarence Major, Christopher Marcus—as well as other careful readers who helped me see "Arroyo" in a new way.

Mahalo to my 'ohana for the hours we spent talking story—Auntie Josephine Manuwai, Uncle Harry and Auntie Ruby Field, Roberta Mejia, Leonard Gonzales, and Jan and Glen Wakamatsu. For her beautiful cover design, thank you to my cousin Puni Kukahiko.

For everything else my mother and father, my sisters and brothers—Noelleen, Myra Ann, Ray, Mike, Pat.

Author Profile

Lisa Gonzales was born in Northern California. As a Jacob K. Javits Fellow, she received her MA in English Literature at the University of California at Davis. Presently she is in the MFA Writing Program at the University of Notre Dame. The stories collected here are from *Hearts of Palm: A Novel in Fados*, her manuscript of linked fiction.